CW00864641

Ruffers, Stink and Topper

The Adventures of Three Rude Rodents

Petra Lloyd

First published in Devon

March 2022

This is a work of fiction. Names, characters, places and events are the product of the author's imagination. Any resemblance to persons, places or rodents is purely coincidental.

Introduction

It could never be said that rats are noted for their charms and good manners. Ruffers was a very large rat indeed with the worst of manners and all in all one of the most foul of creatures on the earth. He liked nothing more than stealing food and he was good at that. Ruffers was a lonely rat though. Read about how he made two very good friends in this delightful book!

This book is dedicated to young readers everywhere. Stop gaming and get reading! It's fun!

Chapter One

Ruffers was born of lowly parents in the dark depths of a sewer in Windlebottom-in-the-Bog, way beneath the hustle and bustle of the busy streets. He was not so much brought up as dragged up by his parents who became rather bored with him when his new brothers and sisters arrived in the family. Thus he was thrown out of the nest to fend for himself and to make his own way in the world without a second glance from them.

Being a rat of great resourcefulness and invention he managed to survive on a diet of curries and chips abandoned beside the bins of a take-away until he was evicted by a rather nosey terrier that was too yappy and nippy for its size. It was not much larger than Ruffers in fact but it made the rodent feel unsafe enough to move on. And so it was that he was forced to move from the city and into the relative safety of the countryside and the peaceful green fields where he feasted on a diet of nuts, berries and the occasional bug.

Since leaving the city he didn't have much in the way of a social life. He was shunned by pigeons, squirrels, foxes and most other rodents and, if truth were told, he was rather lonely. He was not a rat to be beaten though and thought that he might like some friends, but how to set about finding them?

Ruffers pulled at his whiskers and coughed crudely before spitting.

"What to do?" he mused. "I might just form a gang! Then I'll have lots of friends."

He held his nose high in the air and twitched it. He thought that he'd make a fine gang leader.

He'd heard all about gangs from the television news reports and the idea appealed to him, but how should he do so?

After a few moments of not too deep thought he had something of a brainwave.

"I have it! Social media!" and without stopping for a second spit he began to put his thoughts together before adding it to his page.

Gang Members Wanted!

He wrote:

Must have revolting habits, the ability to create havoc and mayhem, must know at least seven really rude words and also like mouldy cheese. Rodents preferred but most other animals considered apart from snakes 'cos I hate them, and ones that might eat me.

"There!" he said. "That should attract my kind of friend."

It was not long before his post was reported left, right and centre, but not before he had received two replies. One was from an old lady called Lillian who informed him that he was a repellent and revolting individual who should be ashamed of himself. This had caused

Ruffers to roll around on the floor crying with laughter and slapping his sides with his paws, but the other was more promising by far.

"My name is Peregrine and I am interested in joining your gang. I know some rude words and rather like cheese although I have not tried it mouldy. I don't think that I have created much havoc or mayhem but am willing to give it a go. With all good wishes,

Master Peregrine Fetherington-Brown, Rat of this Parish."

"Struth, he sounds a possibility, if a bit of a posh git!" said Ruffers. "I suppose he'll do in the absence of any others though."

And so it was that Ruffers and Peregrine became Ratbook friends and arranged to meet that very same day in the hollow oak tree by Cherry Tree Farm.

"Bit of a ruddy misnomer calling it that!" he said aloud. "Should have called it Hollow Oak Tree Farm! That would have been more sensible. Twits, obviously!"

He did not have too long to wait before a rather dapper looking rat appeared. He was wearing a red spotted cravat and a velvet waistcoat and even had a gold pocket watch pinned to one pocket.

"Peregrine's the name," he said, greeting Ruffers with an extended paw. Ruffers took his paw and shook it warmly.

"Well, it's grand to meet you, Pppppper…!"

He tried to say his new friend's name but failed miserably because he was laughing and spluttering too much.

"You can't be in my gang with a name like that!" said Ruffers, sniggering as he tried again to say the name. "Let's think of something more suitable."

"Fine with me, Old Chap!" said Peregrine. "I have never liked it anyway. For a start it's the very devil to spell."

"How did you get your name, by the way?" asked Peregrine.

"Dunno really, but my family were always quite rough, rather common in fact. Folk used to say that the area where we hung out was rough as rats and, somehow, I just got called Ruffers," he explained.

"It suits you I think because you are quite rough. Smelly, no less!" said Peregrine. "Some of my pals call me Perry but it isn't a name that I care for."

They set about making lists of possible names and the results were, to say the least, interesting.

Pongo, Smelly, Stabber, Clubby, Stealer, Hooligan, Stinker and Bum!

They decided that any one of those could fit the bill and thought that the best and fairest way would be to pick one using a pin. Peregrine didn't have a pin but closed his eyes and made a mark on the paper with one claw, and it landed on the name of Stinker.

"I quite like that!" he said. "Hmm… Stinker Fetherington-Brown! That has a certain appeal. It's a sort of flying ace kind of a name, rather like Bomber or Bingo. Chocks away and all that don't you know!"

"It's not bad at all. I like it! I'll call you

Stink for short though," said Ruffers.

And so it was that the two rats cemented their new friendship with a spit on their paws and a shake.

"Two isn't really enough to be a gang," said Stink. "Shall we just be friends?"

"Nah, we can be a gang of two!" said Ruffers.

Chapter Two

The two friends decided that an adventure of some kind was the order of the day. Ruffers thought that they might try to steal something from one of the houses in the nearby village but Stink wasn't at all sure about it.

"It's a mite unwise I fear," he said. "There are quite a few cats living there and they will chase us and jolly well try to kill us. Bad idea, Old Chap!"

"We'll just have to be a bit careful then unless you've got any better ideas," replied Ruffers.

Stink looked thoughtful for a few seconds and then decided that he hadn't so they both set off. As they passed the church that stood on the outskirts of the village they saw a small shape hiding behind one of the grave stones.

"Look!" cried Stink. "A fieldmouse if I'm not mistaken!"

"So it is! Let's get him!" said Ruffers running towards the little animal. "Come on, Stink!"

"Why do we want to get him, Ruffers? He isn't doing any harm there."

"'Cos it'll be fun! We can duff him up a bit," shouted Ruffers, trying to show his mean side.

As they reached the little mouse, who was cowering and looking quite terrified to see two large rodents bearing down on him, they ground to a halt not quite sure of what to do next, never having duffed up anyone or anything before.

"Hello," said the mouse in a trembling tone. "Welcome to my graveyard."

"That's friendly of you and no mistake," said Stink.

"You're very small aren't you?" said Ruffers as he gazed down at the tiny mouse. "Why?"

"It's because I am a fieldmouse and we

are supposed to be small," said the little creature. "It's how we are!"

"What's your name then?" asked Ruffers.

The mouse told him that he was called Topper which caused Ruffers to giggle at what he reasoned was a very silly name for such a tiny thing.

"We were going to duff you up," he said, "but we don't really know how to go about it. Want to join our gang instead?"

"I don't know," answered Topper. "What do you do in your gang?"

"Well, we've only just formed it so we don't really know yet," said Ruffers. "We haven't set out any rules. You can be in it if you like though. Three is a better number for a gang than just two, after all."

"Is there a fee to join?" asked Topper. "I don't have any money at all. Church mice are always very poor."

"No, there's no money involved but you have to know some rude words," said

Ruffers. "Stink knows some which is why I let him join."

Topper looked very pensive.

"We don't really hear any rude words in the church but the man who digs the graves here says quite a few when he gets cross. I could whisper one or two to you if you want."

"Perfect," said Ruffers as he bent down to let the small mouse whisper in his ear.

"Crikey, Topper! Does he really use that sort of language and in a graveyard too? What a very crude fellow he must be! You're in!"

Stink wanted to know what words Topper had whispered, of course, but Ruffers was too embarrassed to repeat them because they were very rude indeed. He thought that he might ask Topper at another time, thinking that they could come in useful if he wanted to insult someone.

"I say, Old Chap, Topper, Old Fruit. We are both a bit peckish. Do you know where one might get some nourishment in these parts, perchance?" asked Stink.

Topper looked puzzled.

"I don't know what you just said. Are you foreign?"

Ruffers decided to translate Stink's question.

"My posh friend wants you to help us to find some nosh! Something to eat! He's not foreign but he just talks funny! "

"Then I'm your mouse!" exclaimed Topper. "Follow me!"

Topper led his two new friends into the church where there was a veritable feast of fine fruit and vegetables, biscuits and packets of all sorts of goodies.

The three rodents began to nibble at a packet of rice, followed by some of the apples, grapes and a packet of chocolate biscuits until they couldn't manage another crumb.

"That was good!" said Ruffers, burping loudly. "Far better than curry and chips!"

With that the gang decided to retire to a quiet corner.

Minutes later there was an almighty scream that echoed around the whole of the church, bouncing off every wall.

"That ruddy mouse has been here again, eating our harvest offerings!"

The scream had come from one of the two flower ladies who had come in to arrange a display for the next service.

"The little beggar!" said the second lady. "Just look what he has done to these biscuits!"

"It wasn't just our church mouse!" said the first one. "There are three of them! Look in this corner! They're curled up asleep."

And indeed they were. All three friends had fallen asleep after enjoying such a feast.

"Where's my broom? I'll soon sort them out, Gladys!" yelled the second lady.

The noise had woken the three rodents who realised that they were in danger and decided to run for it!

They raced towards the open door, chased by the second lady who was yelling still.

The first lady had leapt onto a high chair and was screaming again.

As they ran out of the church Ruffers turned and made a rude gesture and shouted some of the words that he'd learnt from Topper.

They made their way to a corner of the graveyard where they hid under a pile of dried leaves, still rather pleased with themselves. It wasn't long before all three fell asleep once again, this time not to be disturbed by screaming Gladys and her very aggressive companion.

When they awoke it was dark and there was only the faint light of street lamp lighting the corner of the graveyard.

"This is not a safe time for any rodent to go a-walking," said Topper. "There are cats roaming the streets and they are always on the lookout for mice like me."

"We'll sort them out if they dare to try anything like that," said Ruffers waving his front paws wildly in the air.

"No, really, that's a bad idea, Ruffers," said Stink. He'd been chased by cats in the past and it had not ended well.

"See my tail?" he asked. "The end of it is missing. It used to be a goodly inch longer until I was caught by a big ginger tomcat one day. It bit the end off of it and it jolly well hurt I can tell you! I was lucky to have escaped. Cats, like honey badgers, are creatures to be treated with the utmost contempt and no mistake."

The three friends thought it might be a better idea to sneak back into the church to have a midnight feast but the heavy old door had been locked since dusk. Luckily Topper knew another way inside through a small hole that he had nibbled through a door at the back of the building. The gang crept inside and were about to head towards the harvest display when Topper stopped them.

"Do you know about mouse traps?" he asked. Ruffers and Stink shook their heads.

"Well," said Topper. "They are nasty springy things that they set to catch us if we are unlucky enough to tread on them. My great uncle Bert was caught by one a few months ago and I haven't seen him since."

"Best stay clear of them things then!" grunted Ruffers.

Very carefully they headed to the food and began munching at the biscuits again.

"That'll upset Gladys and her daft friend," said Topper. "I've never liked them. They are always grumbling about me and I'm quite harmless really."

Chapter Three

The three friends were up bright and early the following day and were trying to decide on a plan of action for their gang. Ruffers, always thinking about food, wanted to steal cheese from the corner shop. Stink said that he fancied nothing more than a ramble in the fields behind the church and thought it an absolutely spiffing idea.

"What in the name of great steaming dog poo is a spitting idea, Stink?" asked Ruffers, thinking that his pal had flipped.

"Not spitting, you blockhead! Spiffing! It means something rather pleasing. Really, Ruffers, you haven't had much of an education. It's a well-known expression don't you know?" muttered Stink, shaking his head.

Little Topper just looked on and smiled. He decided that his new friends could be quite good company and would make perfect drinking companions too.

"You got any ideas then, Topper?" asked Ruffers.

The mouse thought for a few moments, scratching his head with a front paw.

"Well, I have never been out of the church or the graveyard in my life so both of your suggestions seem good to me," said Topper.

"Ok, then," said Ruffers. "We'll head for the fields and then we can go back to the corner shop to grab some cheese. Sorted!"

With that the three set off along the footpath beside the church to the open fields.

"Wow!" said Topper. "This is a whole new world for me. It's very exciting!"

The sun was shining and there was a warm and gentle breeze blowing. Topper twitched his little whiskers as he sniffed the air. "Everything's very pretty here," he said, thoughtfully. "The flowers look so nice and they smell good too".

He pressed his nose into one and breathed in as deeply as he could. The next moment he was coughing and spluttering and thumping at his chest.

"My goodness, Topper," asked Stink. "Are you all right, Old Chap?"

Ruffers looked at the little mouse and started to laugh at him.

"You great nit!" he said. "You've got pollen all over your face. You look like a greedy bee!"

After some frantic brushing Topper had managed to wipe off most of the sticky pollen and was able to breathe more easily again.

"Some friend you are!" he said, giving Rufffers as cross a look as any fieldmouse could muster. "I thought that I was dying then and all you did was to make silly remarks! Huh!"

"Come along, Topper," said Stink. "I'm sure that he didn't mean to be nasty." He patted his little pal on his back to reassure him.

"Yeah, I did!" said Ruffers. "If he'd have died we could have eaten him. I like a bit of nice juicy steak from time to time. I bet mouse steak is really yummy."

"Yummy or not, we don't eat our friends, Ruffers," said Stink.

"I might," muttered Ruffers under his breath.

"I heard that!" said Topper.

"It looks as if there might be a stream at the bottom of this field," said Stink. "Let's make our way down and you can drink some of the fresh water and wash the remaining pollen from your whiskers too."

"I wouldn't really have eaten you, Topper," said Ruffers.

"Yes, you would!" said the little mouse.

"Yeah, probably would!" muttered Ruffers, chuckling to himself.

Chapter Four

There is only so much that a gang of three rodents can enjoy on country walks and stealing from the corner shop. Enjoying harvest festival offerings is a different matter though and the three friends feasted several more times on the goodies in the church before the food was removed and distributed to the less well-off parishioners.

"We need more adventure in our lives," said Stink one morning. "We're all bright and intelligent creatures and we should be putting our talents to more use, I think."

Ruffers was too busy picking his nose to reply but Topper considered Stink's observation.

"What did you have in mind, Stink?" asked the small mouse.

"I don't quite know as I haven't worked

anything out yet. I'm sure that there is more to life than robbing for food and being rude," mused Stink.

By now Ruffers had stopped picking his nose and had been listening to the conversation.

"Robbing for food and being rude!" he said, echoing Stink's wise words. "You've just made a rhyme, Stink."

Stink thought for a moment.

"Yes, I have!" he exclaimed. "Maybe I should become a poet. Perhaps that is my destiny."

"I wrote a poem once," said Ruffers. "Wanna hear it?"

Stink and Topper nodded as Ruffers cleared his throat and began to recite.

Knickers are red, knickers are blue, some are grubby and smell of.....

"Enough!" yelled Stink. "I can see where your poem is heading and it's rather offensive. Poetry should be nice and gentle, not unpleasant!"

Ruffers looked quite hurt. He had been very proud of his verse.

"Full marks for trying though, Ruffers, Old Fellow," said Stink, seeing that his friend was upset. Topper was still rolling around on the ground laughing.

"Well, I liked it!" he said.

Chapter Five

Stink thought more about the idea of becoming a poet over the next few days but didn't really come up with anything. He liked the suggestion though.

"To be a poet I would need pens, paper and a desk. If I had a desk I would need somewhere to keep it under cover. My work would become damp otherwise and would be spoilt, as would my desk. Fine furniture should be housed in a fine home, don't you know!"

"Blimey, Stink!" said Ruffers. "You don't like to do things by halves do you? Wot you got in mind then?"

"Leave it with me!" said Stink.

"Perhaps we should make up some rules for our gang," said Ruffers. "All gangs need rules!"

"I think that is an excellent idea, Ruffers," Stink replied.

"I'm just happy to be in your gang, Ruffers," said little Topper. "I didn't have any friends when I lived in the churchyard. Even the grave digger man used to shout at me!"

"You suggested some rules when you sent out that message on your Ratbook page looking for gang members," Stink reminded him. "They had to know rude words and like eating mouldy cheese I believe."

"Yes, that's true," said Ruffers. "Those can be our first rules then. Let's add some more!"

"I think that we should have a rule that we are kind to each gang member," said Topper.

"Ok, that's a good one," said Ruffers. "We can be as horrid as we like to anyone who is not in our gang but we can't be horrid to our own members. Agreed?"

"Well......," muttered Stink, who was about to disagree, thinking that it might be rather mean.

"Sorted!" said Ruffers. "I'm the leader so I agree!"

Stink and Topper had several more ideas about rules but Ruffers did not like any of them. He especially hated the one about letting more members join and he was perfectly happy with the gang as it was. He liked his two new friends and thought that any more members might upset the balance of things.

There didn't seem much point in trying to add more suggestions as Ruffers always had the final decision anyway. Stink and Topper thought that it was best to let him have his way, for now.

Chapter Six

The three friends decided to take another walk, this time to the wild wood where they could enjoy running through the piles of dried leaves and eating the last of the season's blackberries.

They made their way out of the village, through the fields and then along an old track that led to the wood. As they passed a pair of very large and old iron gates Stink paused.

"Behind these gates is a somewhat splendid home where a rather rich relative of mine used to live," he said. "I don't know if anyone lives there now. It could be just the place for a poet and his desk."

"One way to find out!" said Topper.

"Let's go to the wild wood first and then we can explore behind these gates on our way back," said Ruffers, being quite bossy as usual.

Ruffers, Stink and Topper didn't find any blackberries worth eating in the wild wood but they did have fun running in and out of the piles of dead leaves that had fallen beneath the trees. Topper found some cobnuts that were dry and ready to nibble though. After enjoying some of those the three rodents set off once again to see what lay behind the gates that they had passed earlier.

It was a fair way to walk to the old house once they had sneaked through the big gates but, eventually, they arrived.

"Looks a bit of a wreck!" said Ruffers as he surveyed the place.

There was ivy growing over the walls and some of the window panes were either cracked or missing.

"It used to be a rather fine mansion when I knew it first. The owners were Lord and Lady somebody, I forget the name, and they had lots of staff. My second cousin twice removed lived here with his family." explained Stink.

"So they didn't own it, Stink?" asked Topper.

"My goodness no, but they lived here for many years, mostly in the staff kitchens. I don't know what became of them because they stopped corresponding a while ago," he replied.

"What does corresponding mean?" asked Topper.

"Oh, you know, sending letters and emails, that sort of thing!" explained Stink as he smoothed his long whiskers and twitched his tail. "Let's go inside."

Ruffers tried to push open the heavy old front door.

"Give us a hand, you two," he called.

All three rodents pushed hard and managed to open it just enough to squeeze through.

"I don't think that anyone lives here now," said Topper as he looked around the hallway. "Just look at all these spiders' webs and dust!"

The old place looked very empty and neglected.

"We can hang out here for a while," said Ruffers.

"Indeed we can," agreed Stink. "There isn't anyone to chase us away."

"We'll be warm and dry too," said little Topper who didn't really like the cold weather at all.

"This can be our home now," said Ruffers, who had always wanted a proper den of his own.

"Yes, I suppose it can," agreed Stink, who had always had a notion to own a mansion. "I shall call it Stink Towers!"

"Stink Towers? Stink Towers? Why should we get to name it after you, Stinker Fetherington-Brown?" yelled Ruffers, angrily.

He only ever used Stink's full name when he was cross.

"Because I am the rat who found it, that is why!" Stink replied. "So it seems only right and proper that it should be named after me, so there, Ruffers, Old Thing!"

He could be quite haughty at times.

Ruffers thought for a few moments. Perhaps his friend was right but he didn't much like the idea and decided to come up with a better name.

"What about Ruffers Rat Towers?" he asked.

"OK, maybe," said Stink, who didn't really want to fall out about the matter.

Little Topper did not want to be left out of the naming game either.

"I would like to propose that we call it Topper Towers," he said.

Both rats thought for a few moments longer.

"Do you know," said Stink, "but that's actually a jolly fine name. Topper Towers, eh? I like it! It's splendid and no mistake!"

"Huh! Topper Towers indeed!" grunted Ruffers, who secretly thought it a fine name too. "OK, if we must!"

The tiny mouse was so delighted that he ran around chanting *We live in Topper Towers, we live in Topper Towers* over and over at the top of his voice.

Chapter Seven

Life in Topper Towers was much nicer than living out in the open air, even if it wasn't very gang-like. The three rodents were warm and dry and felt far safer than before with no cats to bother them.

They had been exploring in every room of the place and Stink was absolutely thrilled to have found his way to the nursery where there was a large and very old dolls house. He wasn't a rat that played with dolls, of course, but he found a rather fine desk inside, complete with a chair that swivelled, and it even had tiny pencils and sheets of notepaper in the drawers on one side.

"Just what a fine poet such as myself needs!" he said.

He decided that it would be best positioned in one of the large rooms on the ground floor of the house where they spent most of their time.

Very carefully he and Ruffers had managed to carry it all the way down the long staircases and put it in its new position. Topper had been too small to help so he just watched from a safe distance.

"Now to work!" said Stink. "I have always enjoyed the writings of Wordsworth, Betjeman and Tennyson. Perhaps the name of Fetherington-Brown will be added to this list soon."

Ruffers had been listening and thought that his friend had lost his senses. He wasn't pleased that Stink had thought his own poem about knickers rude either. He decided that he might write some more verses of his own.

Stink spent many hours over the next few days and nights composing his poetry until he had a folio of his best works ready to be submitted to a book publisher. He thought that he would read them to Ruffers and Topper first, so one evening they all gathered around Stink's desk to enjoy his writings. Stink cleared his throat and introduced his first poem.

I was a rather lonely rat
Until I made two friends.
And now I'm not a lonely rat.
Signed Stink the rat.
The end.

Ruffers and Topper stared at each other in disbelief. They were not at all impressed with Stink's first poem.

"Read us another, please!" said Topper who thought that they could only improve.

"Will do! Glad that you enjoyed it, Topper, my old chum," said Stink as he prepared to read another.

"The sun was shining on my fur," began Stink.

"This one might be better than your first one, Stink," said Ruffers. "That one was rubbish!"

"Please don't interrupt me, Ruffers," said

Stink, looking a little annoyed. "You will spoil the artistry of my work. I'll begin again!"

"Artistry, my great big bottom!" laughed Ruffers heartily at the notion that Stink's poem might be described as artistry.

He thought that it was the biggest pile of literary poo ever. He didn't want to be too rude though so he stuffed a paw into his mouth to stifle any more of his sniggering.

Stink began a second time.

The sun was shining on my fur
It made me feel so warm.
I hate it when my fur is wet.
This happens in a storm.

Ruffers and Topper tried very hard not to laugh as Stink read out more of his verses but they couldn't contain their mirth and soon both of them were rolling around on the floor holding their sides.

"You two do not appreciate fine poetry!" grunted Stink. "I shall submit them to the best publisher that I can find and then you won't find it so funny when I become famous."

With that Stink decided to go outside for a walk around the gardens.

"I wish to be alone!" he said, trying to sound dramatic. "I may be some time!"

He twitched his whiskers, swished his tail and muttered a loud *Huh!* as he left the room.

"I think that we have upset him, Ruffers," said Topper. "I didn't mean to. It's just that his poems were so bad."

"They were terrible!" replied Ruffers.

Chapter Eight

Stink wrote several more poems over the next week, each one as bad as all of the others. He spent some time looking for a suitable publisher too and eventually decided to send them to one that was requesting submissions for an anthology to be called *Poetry Now*.

He thought that he would send an email, enclosing his best verses and spent the next hour writing it and adding ten of what he considered to be his finest ones.

"My work is done!" he announced.

He wandered off to find the others and before long all three were sitting in the gardens chatting happily together.

Stink had tired himself out with all of his writings and soon he fell asleep and started to snore gently.

"Let's go and see what he's been up to!" whispered Ruffers to Topper.

"Good plan, Ruffers!" Topper whispered back, not wanting to awaken their sleepy friend.

They both crept back into the house where they found Stink's email to the publishing house, still open at his desk.

"Struth, Topper," said Ruffers. "He really is going to send his bad poems off. He'll be very upset when they tell him that they are no good."

"Yes, he'll be very sad," said the little mouse. "He was proud of them."

"I know!" said Ruffers with a glint in his eye. "I am going to add some of my own to his email and then press *send.*"

"I liked the one about knickers," said Topper.

"Me too," said Ruffers as he typed furiously. "I'll add that one and a few more as well, 'cos I've made up loads of them."

"Do you like this one?" asked Ruffers, still

typing. He coughed and then spat to prepare himself in readiness to recite his poem.

There once was a duckling called Will
Whose farting made everyone ill.
His friends tried to stop 'em
With a cork up his bottom
But that just made him burp through his bill.

"That's brilliant!" giggled Topper. "Far funnier than Stink's efforts!"

Ruffers added four more of his rude verses and then pressed the *send* button before heading back to the gardens where they found Stink, still sleeping.

"Don't tell him what you've done, Ruffers," said Topper.

"No chance!" said Ruffers. "He'd be very cross indeed!"

Stink had been woken by his friends' chattering and wanted to know who would be very cross indeed.

Ruffers thought for a moment and then told him that he was talking about a hedgehog that they had passed by the wall earlier. "I stole his apples while he slept!" lied Ruffers.

"Apples, eh? Did you keep one for me? I love apples!" said Stink.

"Sorry, no, we ate them all," said Topper.

"Mean of you!" muttered Stink before falling asleep once more.

Chapter Nine

Stink was busy reading his emails the following day when he was delighted to find one from the publishing company. Excitedly he called to Ruffers and Topper to come and listen as he began to read:

Dear Master Stinker Fetherington-Brown. We received your poetry submissions yesterday which were read by a member of our team.

"See how quickly they have responded?" he said. "They must be very keen to publish my work." He read on:

*Sadly we do not consider your first ten poems to be worthy of publication in our anthology, **Poetry Now**. We did not see any merit whatsoever in those. We did enjoy the further six poems though and would like to include them in the new edition of our series of **Rude Verses for Rude Readers** as we consider these to eminently suitable. We are sure that our* *readers will enjoy them very much. We found the one about knickers particularly good.*

With all good wishes

E. Duckstein

Earnest Duckstein of Duckstein Publishers.

"Knickers?" yelled Stink. "Knickers? What have you two been up to? I didn't send that dreadfully rude knickers poem of yours, Ruffers! Nor did I send any other rude ones. Which of you was responsible for this? I demand to know!"

Stink looked very funny as he danced around the room yelling. His face had turned bright red and he looked angry.

"Sorry, Stink, but you left your email message open so we decided to have some fun by adding more poems before we sent it," said Ruffers.

"Don't blame me, Ruffers!" said little Topper. "It was all your idea!"

"Well yes it was, but they liked my poetry and want to publish it. All of it! That's a result isn't it, Stink?" said Ruffers, trying to calm the situation.

Stink thought for a moment, then a second moment and then a third.

"Well, as I see it, Ruffers, Old Flower," said Stink. "They liked your stuff and not mine. I am upset, of course, but perhaps I am not cut out to be a poet after all."

"We can't all be great writers, Stink," said Ruffers.

"That's not really helping matters," said Topper. "Poor Stink is upset that they didn't want his verses."

"I am rather disappointed," said Stink. "On the other hand, I would not have liked my works to have been published by a firm that offers a book of rude verses for rude readers so perhaps it is just as well that they rejected them."

Ruffers agreed that they had not been the right publisher for his friend's poetry and suggested that he might send them to another firm for consideration.

"No," replied Stink, being rather dramatic again. "One just cannot face more rejection."

"Then perhaps 'one' would care for a mug of acorn coffee," said Ruffers, imitating his posh friend.

Stink nodded and soon all three were sitting down together sipping mugs of the steaming brew.

"There is one good thing about it though," said Topper. "Won't you get paid for the rude poems?"

"Yes, you're right!" said Stink." "I will message a reply accepting their offer as soon as I have finished my drink."

"They were my poems, Matey," said Ruffers. "So the money will be mine too. Don't you try to steal it!"

"They were sent under my name, Ruffers, Old Fellow. We will share it I think," said

Stink.

Ruffers agreed that was only fair, and continued to slurp his coffee before burping very loudly.

Chapter Ten

The little gang had been puzzled in the past few days by strange noises coming from the attic.

"Perhaps Topper Towers is haunted," said Topper.

"Nah, probably just birds nesting up there, or bats maybe," said Ruffers.

"There were bats in the church where I used to live," said Topper. "They were never noisy. I never heard as much as a squeak from any of them so I don't think it is bats."

"It might be squirrels," said Stink. "I believe that they like climbing into roof spaces and attics."

"We should investigate!" said Ruffers. "We don't want any ne'er-do-wells invading our home!"

The three friends made their way to the attic room.

"I hope it isn't ghosts," said Topper. "Ghosts are scary!"

"It won't be ghosts, you great oaf," said Ruffers. "They aren't real anyway."

Very carefully he turned the knob and the old door creaked loudly as it swung open.

"Who are you lot and what are you a-doing are in my attic?" asked a rather gruff voice.

They peered into the darkness but couldn't make out who or what had spoken.

"Well, my name is Ruffers Rat, this is my friend, Stinker Fetherington-Brown, he is a rat too, and the little one is Topper. He isn't a rat because he is too small. He's just a fieldmouse," explained Ruffers.

"Well, Ruffers Rat, you are in my room. Get out!" snarled the gruff voice. "And take your friends with you!"

"No, you are in our home, whoever you are!" said Ruffers. "You can get out!"

Stink wasn't at all pleased to have another creature living in Topper Towers.

"Come out and show yourself!" he said.

The creature made its way to the open door and they could see that it was another rat, quite large and a darker colour than Ruffers.

"Right, you three!" said the rat. "This is my attic and that's all about it."

"No, we suggest that you leave our attic," said Stink who was beginning to lose his temper.

"We don't want to share our home with a rat like you," said Topper, trying to sound ferocious but failing miserably.

"I'm not here on my own," said the intruder rat. "There is a huge army of us up here, ready to spring into action at a moment's notice so don't try anything!"

Ruffers thought for a moment, not quite sure of what was to be done.

"Let's make our way downstairs to our

own quarters again and we can talk strategies," he told his two pals.

"This is not over, rat!" he shouted as angrily as he could.

Once they were back in the sitting room downstairs they mused on the situation.

"I don't really mind them being there," said Topper. "Apart from a little bit of noise we don't really hear them."

Stink said that he didn't really mind either but that Topper Towers was their home and they were there uninvited.

Ruffers said that they had no right to be there anyway and that, if they were allowed to stay, they should all be paying rent to him. He thought that they would be smelly too and that they might hold large and noisy parties late into the nights. It would not do.

After more discussion the three rodents agreed that they didn't want them living in their home but that they could live outside in the gardens as long as they were well away from the house.

"How will we get them to move?" asked Topper.

All three remained deep in thought for a few minutes longer.

"I have it!" declared Stink. "We didn't much care for the rustling noises that they made in the attic so we might make lots of noise here and drive them out!"

"That's a good plan, Stink," said Ruffers, wishing that he had thought of it himself.

"Saucepan lids and metal spoons make a big noise," said Topper. "I could bang them together right outside of the attic."

"We could all do that, Topper," said Stink. "Let's go for it!"

And so it was that all three rodents armed themselves with the biggest pans that they were able to carry, along with large metal spoons. Once they reached the attic again they placed their pans on the floor and began bashing them with the spoons and with all of their might

It wasn't long before the door was flung open and the intruder rat came out yelling.

"What the flip is all the noise for?" he demanded. "All we want is some peace and some quiet. Stop the racket, won't you?"

"Not a chance!" shouted Ruffers, above the din. "We will keep this up until you leave our home. We have decided that you can all go to live in the gardens, so there!"

"Keep it up, lads!" he said to his two friends.

All three of them kept on hammering on the pans as loudly as they could, even though their arms were starting to ache quite badly.

It was almost three hours later when a troupe of rats or various sizes emerged from the attic room with their paws in their ears.

"We can't take any more of this," said one old rat. "We have decided to take you up on your offer of letting us live in the gardens."

And with that they all began to wend their ways down the stairs and out of the front door, with Ruffers, Stink and Topper behind them, still beating their pans loudly.

Once the last of them had left the house they slammed the door and turned the key in the lock.

"I don't think that we will be troubled by them anymore," said Stink.

"I think you're right," agreed Ruffers.

"My ears are ringing!" sighed little Topper.

Chapter Eleven

The next few days were bright and sunny and the three rodents enjoyed playing in the gardens.

"I think that those invading rats have gone away," said Ruffers. "They are nowhere to be seen now."

What they did not know was that they had not left. Far from it! They had started to burrow under the house where they had been busy making a huge den for themselves.

They had dug busily for many hours until there was a large cavern below Topper Towers. They had added piles of dead leaves and straw to make it cosy too.

And so it was that Ruffers and his two friends and all of the rival rats lived in peace and harmony both inside and below Topper Towers, unbeknown to each other.

One morning as Ruffers, Stink and

Topper were enjoying a lazy breakfast they heard a strange sound, a kind of long and low growl.

"That sounded like thunder!" said Topper, who was rather afraid of storms.

"Don't be daft, Topper," said Ruffers. "It needs to be raining to have thunder and it isn't. It was probably Stink's tummy rumbling."

"Indeed it was not!" said Stink. "It was far too loud to have been any of my internal organs. How very discourteous of you, Ruffers!"

"There it is again!" cried Topper. "I'm going to go outside to take a look."

The noises grew louder as Topper looked around to see where they were coming from. They seemed to be from the old house itself, which confused the little mouse.

Just then there was an even louder noise and a cracking sound from one of the downstairs windows. Topper watched as the glass broke and fell from the frame onto the ground below, narrowly missing him. This was followed by a lot more creaking, and then a large crack appeared in the wall beside the front door. Topper ran back inside to warn Ruffers and Stink of what was happening to their home.

"You need to get outside very quickly," he cried. "The house is starting to collapse."

All three raced outside as fast as their legs could carry them and began to run into the garden as stones and bricks continued to fall from Topper Towers creating a massive cloud of dust.

"Blimey, Stink, this is a disaster!" said Ruffers. "Perhaps there's been an earthquake close by."

"I don't know what else would have caused our house to fall to bits," said Stink. "It is a disaster and no mistake!"

"Can you see Topper?" asked Ruffers. "I can't see him and he was following behind us as we ran out of the house."

Ruffers and Stink began to call out Topper's name but he was nowhere to be seen.

"I do hope he's ok," said Stink. "I'm a bit worried about him."

Just then a very dusty shape appeared. It wasn't little Topper but the intruder rat.

"Help me! Please help me!" gasped the rat. My fellow rats are trapped under your home and they can't escape."

"We think that we've had an earthquake," said Ruffers.

The intruder rat looked very sheepish.

"Er, I don't think that there has been an earthquake. After you threw us out of your attic we decided to make a home under your house. We've been busy burrowing there for ages and I think we overdid it," he explained.

"What!!!!!!!!" shouted Ruffers. "So your burrowing has destroyed our home! You idiots! You total and complete and utter nincompoops!"

"I'm really sorry," said the rat. "We didn't mean it to happen. We just wanted somewhere cosy to live."

"I suppose that we were living there without anyone's permission if truth be told," said Stink. "We just moved in because it was uninhabited."

"That doesn't help my fellow rats to escape though," said the intruder rat. "Please, please will you both help them?"

"They are our fellow creatures, Ruffers," said Stink. "We should help them really."

"I suppose we should," said Ruffers. "First we must find Topper though. He's lost somewhere."

"I'll help you to find that little mouse if you will help me in return. Deal?" asked the intruder rat.

They all agreed and began calling Topper's name as they looked for him.

There was so much rubble and dust around that it made the search difficult but all three rodents scrambled over the piles of fallen stones and bricks in their quest. Before long Stink thought that he heard a very small voice crying for help somewhere below one pile of stones.

"Is that you, Topper?" he asked.

There was more crying from the little mouse, which was trapped and quite terrified.

"Can you help me?" he asked in a trembling voice. "My back foot is stuck and it hurts. I've tried to pull myself free and I can't do it."

There were so many big stones above where Topper was trapped that it seemed an impossible task but they had to rescue their friend.

"We are going to need more help," said Ruffers. "We can't do it by ourselves."

The intruder rat had an idea and explained to Ruffers and Stink that if they could rescue his fellow rats they might all be able to assist in the rescue of Topper.

"It's a kind offer," said Stink. "We weren't very kind to you and your friends when you were living in our attic. We don't even know your name."

"It's Rover! Pleased to meet you!" said the intruder rat.

"Rover?" asked Stink. "But that's a name for a dog."

"My parents wanted a pet dog but that's beside the point at this present moment," said Rover. "We need to rescue everyone."

Chapter Twelve

The three rats went to survey the scene and it was a very sorry sight to behold. Most of the front section of the house had fallen to the ground, and also into the large cavern below which the rat colony had made.

"There might be a way out if they can make their way to the back of their cave," said Stink. "I know that there is a wine cellar there. If they can burrow through to it they could crawl out easily."

"Maybe we could go into the house from the other side and climb down into the cellar. Then you will be able to shout to your rat pack what they should do," said Ruffers.

"It's worth trying," said Rover.

Soon they were in the wine cellar hammering on the back wall to get the attention of the other rats.

"We're in here! Can you hear us?" shouted Rover.

"Yes!" shouted one of the trapped rats "Can you get us out?"

The rats had all raced to the back of their den when the house had started to collapse and there was not much room for them there.

Ruffers and Stink looked at the walls of the cellar and thought that they seemed very solid and thick.

Rover was tapping at the stonework. "This one feels as if it might be loose," he said, pointing to one of the lower stones.

"Indeed it does!" said Stink. "We need to prize it out."

Ruffers remembered that there was a pickaxe in one of the greenhouses and hurried off to fetch it.

Soon he was back in the wine cellar and all three rats began trying to slide the edge of the axe under the loose stone. It was surprisingly easy to move it out of place. Rover began to pick away at the soil where it had been and soon he had managed to break through to the rat den.

"Rover!" called one old rat. "You've rescued us. We knew you would."

They clawed away at the soil from both sides of the small opening and soon they had made a hole large enough for the trapped rats to crawl through.

"We aren't done yet," said Ruffers. "We need to help our friend, Topper. He's trapped under a pile of stones and can't get out."

A few of the larger rats agreed to help to rescue Topper and they carried the pickaxe around to what was left of the front of the house and to the pile of stones that had trapped the little mouse.

"Can you hear us, Topper?" called Ruffers. "We are here with some new friends to get you out."

He called again to his little friend but there was no reply.

"I do hope that's he's ok," said Stink. "We could hear him crying earlier."

The rats began their work, rolling the heavy stones out of the way and shovelling piles of dirt and dust with their cupped paws. They worked long and hard for at least two hours until Ruffers could see a very small claw between two of the smaller stones.

"He's here!" called Ruffers as he crawled down to stroke it.

There was no reply but the tiny claw twitched just a little. "And he is still alive!" he said.

Very carefully they managed to move the last of the stones that were trapping the mouse. Topper was lying there, eyes closed and covered in dust but he was breathing still. Ruffers managed to lift him out and, very gently, he passed him up to Stink before climbing out himself.

Poor Topper was quite bruised and one of his back paws had been bleeding. He whimpered a little as he opened his eyes very slowly.

"Where am I?" he asked in a tiny voice.

"Don't worry, Topper," said Stink. "There has been an accident but you're safe now."

"It was no accident, Stink," grumbled Ruffers. "Those stupid rats burrowed under Topper Towers and they destroyed it and that's a fact!"

"They didn't mean that to happen, Ruffers, Old Chap," said Stink. "Perhaps we were at fault in not letting them live in our home. It would have been big enough, don't you know."

Ruffers and Stink carried their friend into the back of the house where the rooms had not been damaged. Ruffers fetched a blanket and wrapped it around Topper's little body to make him warm and Stink bathed Topper's back paw before bandaging it. The mouse was shivering and his ears and nose were very pale.

"You know, Ruffers, that we could not have been able to rescue Topper without the help from Rover's friends," said Stink. "He'd have died. Maybe we should be kinder to them."

"Ok, maybe we should," agreed Ruffers.

Chapter Thirteen

Topper had been very upset after his accident but before too many days had passed he was feeling much better. Soon he was running around the gardens happily once more.

Ruffers and Stink decided that, although gang warfare might be fun, it was far nicer being kind to their fellow creatures, apart from cats and honey badgers, of course. Neither rat had ever seen a honey badger but they had heard all about them and knew that they were to be feared.

They had made friends with Rover's rat pack and, after a lot of work rebuilding Topper Towers, they had all decided to live there together peacefully rather than to fight one another.

Rover knew quite a lot about gardening, and growing tasty things to eat too, and the old greenhouses were soon overflowing with all sorts of beans and peas as well as berries of all colours.

Stink gave up all ideas of becoming a famous poet. Instead he found a real talent for painting and made some fine portraits of his new friends, as well as of Ruffers and Topper. These were hung proudly in the rebuilt hall for all to see and admire, and Topper Towers became a lively and exciting place to be.

They had lots of visitors with family members travelling from far and wide to stay there. Ruffers was very good at tracking down old and long lost friends and families of Rover's pack using Ratbook, and so the house was never short of good company as well as good food.

"Social Media is a wonderful thing," he mused one morning as he sat enjoying coffee with Stink and Topper. "If I hadn't asked for some new friends all of those months ago I would never have found you two."

"You didn't ask for new friends, Ruffers" said Stink. "You actually wanted members for your new gang."

"So I did!" agreed a reformed and slightly embarrassed Ruffers.

Topper reminded him that they needed to know some rude words and like eating mouldy cheese as well.

They thought that life in Topper Towers was a million miles away from their escapades in the church when they ate their way through the harvest festival food and were chased by the flower ladies.

Now they had dozens of new friends and even Ruffers had decided that the members of Rover's pack were nice, although he was still the leader of the gang, of course.

"I want us all to stay friends for ever and ever!" said Topper.

"Well, I want that too, and I want to live here in Topper Towers for ever and ever!" added Stink.

"You great pair of drips!" laughed Ruffers, who, secretly, wanted those things as well.

The End

Dear Reader,

If you have enjoyed reading this book please leave a review on Amazon. Thank you.

Petra Lloyd

Printed in Great Britain
by Amazon